Stories of Old Ireland
for
Children

EDMUND LENIHAN

ILLUSTRATED BY
Frances Boland

MERCIER PRESS

MERCIER PRESS
PO Box 5, 5 French Church Street, Cork
and
16 Hume Street, Dublin 2

Trade enquiries to CMD Distribution
55a Spruce Avenue, Stillorgan Industrial Park, Blackrock, Dublin

© E. Lenihan, 1986

ISBN 0 85342 927 8

A CIP is available for this book from the British Library.

15 14 13 11 12 11 10 9 8 7 6

Printed in Ireland by Colour Books Ltd.

Contents

Fionn Mac Cumhail and the Feathers from China

Long ago in Ireland – in spite of what people think nowadays – there were men who used to travel to the four ends of the world, and few travelled farther than Fionn and the men of the Fianna in their various hunts and adventures. One of those who did, however, was Maeldún, who went sailing the seven seas of the earth searching for something (no one knows what) and didn't find it in the end. But he and his men found many other things, which were much more valuable to them entirely. They brought home strange stories about a land at the other side of the world called China, where all the people could write, and write backwards into the bargain. But none of these stories was stranger than the one about how the Chinese used to punish those people who did wrong.

* * * * *

One night a feast was going on strong in the banqueting hall of Tara – great merriment, noise, laughter and all the rest of it – but King Cormac was sitting morosely in the middle of it all, his head between his hands.

'Ohh! All the stories that are here, I have them all heard before, and I'm sick of it. If there was only some new man who could tell me something I didn't hear already I'd be happy. And he'd be rich!'

Fionn and Diarmaid were full of sympathy for his highness for they knew how much he loved stories, but there was nothing they could do and they knew it. Cormac had, indeed, heard them all, old and new, good and bad. Suddenly, over the noise of the merrymaking, pounding was heard on the front door.

'Open that, quick,' said Cormac, but without too much hope. 'It might be a stranger with a new story.'

The door was thrown open and in strode a tall sunburnt man.

'God save you, your highness,' he said, bowing.

'God save yourself, and who are you, at all? If you have a story for us this night you're the guest of honour, because we're starved for a fresh tale!'

8

'Hah! Story, is it? That's the very thing I have, and a story ye didn't hear the like of before, either,' said the stranger confidently.

'Aha! My prayers are answered. Bring him a bite to eat, quick, so he can start the telling!' said Cormac. No storyteller would ever be asked to perform in Ireland at that time without getting a meal first. So, they sat him down, brought him anything he wanted and let him eat it in peace. After that was done the men of the Fianna settled themselves down on their elbows and gazed at him, waiting to hear what wonderful scenes and visions would come from his mouth. If they were half as good as he claimed they must be extraordinary, indeed, because the stories that the court of King Cormac hadn't heard could be counted twice over on one hand. Anyone who wanted to make his or her name at the storytelling would face for Tara where the High King lived – so much so that there was often a queue of seanchchaís (storytellers) waiting to get in, to make their fortune, as each and every one of them thought. Few fortunes had been made, up to this night, in any case.

When the last of the crockery had been cleared away and only the drinking-goblets glimmered on the tables the stranger settled himself back comfortably in his seat, took out his pipe and a fist of dried buacháláns *(ragwort)* – no tobacco in those days, and better off without it too – looked slowly from face to face surrounding him and began:

'I was on a ship. . . a short while ago. . . and we're not home so long at all. An' where we went to, now,' he said, puffing his pipe as he remembered, ''twas a place called China.'

'Ohh! Begor!' said the men. 'Where's that? Is it anywhere west of Inis na Rón?'

'No,' he said. ''Tis in the other direction entirely. We got there by accident, and I don't rightly know *how* we got there because it was dark most of the way and we slept a good deal of the time. The rest of it was lightning and thunder, and 'twas blowing us places we didn't want to go at all. For a finish, we didn't care where we came to land as long as 'twas dry enough for us to get off the ship because we were wet and worn from it.'

'Hu-hoo!' cried the men of the Fianna, 'that's the only kind of a journey to go on, 'cos you'll always find interesting things when you're expecting nothing.'

'Oh, faith, 'twas interesting all right. But many's the day and night of that journey and the wind blowing us nearly away from ourselves, when we wished and prayed to be back in our beds in the holy land of Ireland.'

'Not a bad place to be, at all, surely,' said Conán Maol, 'but come on! What about the country of China – or whatever you call it?'

He took another pull on his pipe and continued.

'Well, the people were small, with yellow skin, and they'd look at you fierce and strange. And they all had tails out of the back of their heads.'

'Oh, by the power of Bel, what class of people were they, at all? Would they bite you?' cried the listeners.

'No. But wait till I tell ye. Usedn't the women there dress like the men, and the men like the women!'

'Aghh! That must be a terrible place, all right. They couldn't be good and they to be like that. But tell us more!'

'They had strange big animals waiting for us when we came out of the ship, with two humps on their backs, and we had to perch ourselves above on one of those humps while the driver perched on the other one. Off we went then, and well I remember it 'cos it nearly crippled me.'

'Had they a name on them animals?' asked

Goll Mac Morna.

'Camels they called them,' said he.

The men of Ireland knew nothing about camels at that time, never even having heard the name, so it made a big impression. Round the tables it went, from man to man, each one rolling the word up and down in his mouth as if he were sucking marbles, every one of them manufacturing his own story out of this new thing for telling in some other house at some time: 'I met this man who was in a place called China, and he travelled on an animal called a camel – could you believe such a thing? . . .' and so on.

But the stranger was speaking again, and every man put his private dreams carefully away for the moment to listen.

'We travelled across the land of China, and the sun, 'twould fry your brains because there wasn't a stem of greenery in the whole place.'

The men of the Fianna, naturally, didn't think much of a place that hadn't grass, and plenty of it, but when they heard that there were no woods or chirping birds they began to feel that this was not the place for them, even if they could have seen it.

'Man, there was only rock and stones and sand; then more rocks and sand and stones,' he continued.

'And what did ye do for drinks?' asked a voice from the audience.

'Our tongues got as big as turnips inside our mouths. But that wasn't the most annoying bit! What broke my heart entirely was to see the camels, when we'd come to one of the few pools of water in that place, looking around them stupidly. Not a bit of a worry on them whether they got water or not! I thought 'twas magic until I found out later on that camels keep a big supply of water inside the very same humps where we were sitting as dry as sticks.'

'Eee!' cried the men of the Fianna, gazing in wonder at each other. 'Could you believe him at all? It sounds like a pack of lies, but 'tis a great story. Hi! Tell us more!'

'We kept going for thirty solid days and thirty nights,' said he, 'and at night there'd be icicles hanging off your nose, but in the morning 'twould be frying your skull again. 'Twas that kind of weather.'

'Oh, holy Crom, isn't it fierce. Tell us more.'

'At the end of thirty days, travelling every day full blast, we came to a wall, for all the world like the wall of a dún *(fort)*, only bigger. There were towers along it, and men guarding it, and above on top of it, to make it all worse,

wasn't there a road.'

'A thiarna milis!' they groaned. 'Worse and worse indeed! But talk away, anyway.'

'Well, we climbed up onto the wall – there was a ladder up to one of the towers – and they even had a place for bringing up the camels, too, and no sooner were they up than off we went along the wall. We marched that road for thirty more days but we weren't coming to the end of it. On and on and on it went. . .'

'Ah, here, are you telling us lies?'

'Not a lie in it,' said he. 'Up the sides of mountains went the road, down into huge valleys, across great plains. . .'

'As big as the Bog of Allen?' asked someone from the crowd.

The stranger looked towards the voice, pity in his voice.

'Compared to those plains the Bog of Allen is only a pool of mud for frogs to cool themselves in.'

No man took that as an insult. Each was too intent on hearing what followed.

'We came at last to the sea, and there the road on the wall ended.' Relief showed on every face.

'But the road didn't finish there!'

Men looked at each other in wonder, but before any questions could be asked he continued:

'On the sea, stretching as far as our eyes could see, were ships, as many as a man could count in a year and a day.'

'What class of ships?' croaked Liagán Luaimneach.

'Square ships the like of which we never saw before, with pictures painted on their sails, and a little house like a small dún at the stern.'

'Ah, here! Are you trying to tell us that they had dúns floating in the sea?'

'I am not. They were ships all right, because the next thing we did was to drive the camels over a timber bridge and onto the ship nearest the shore. From that on we were able to ride the camels for three days over the decks of the ships, out and out to sea with never a stop. When we came to the last ship there was no trace of any land before us or around us so we looked in the only other place there could be land – straight down – and sure enough, below us in the green water we saw a city, with people going about their business.'

'C'mere now,' said Cormac, shifting nervously in his seat, 'don't try to tell me ye went down there.'

'That's the very thing we did. But if 'twas left to ourselves we'd be still there looking at it. No! 'Twas the camels had the courage – or the stupidity, I don't know. At any rate, they walked over the side of the last ship, one after the other, in spite of anything the drivers could do, and made no attempt whatsoever to swim. I closed my eyes and said my prayers, thinking I was surely drowned. I held my breath, felt myself going down and down, and when my eyes popped open at last from the lack of air they nearly fell out o' my head entirely when I saw where we were.'

'But don't keep us here and *our* eyes on stalks!' clamoured the Fianna. 'Tell us! Tell us!'

'Safe and sound inside a big bubble. Dry land

under the sea.'

No one could think of anything to ask except, 'What were the people like down there?'

'The same type, with the same gimp on them as the first crowd we met. But listen now, 'cos 'tis here the interesting story starts,' he winked.

'Hold on a second, now, for a minute!' said Cormac in a shocked voice, 'until we fill up the drinking-cups again. This is fierce thirsty work.'

There was a blast of hugger-mugger around the hall for a few minutes, until the glass of poitín, wine or whatever each man was having, was filled. Then they settled themselves again when they saw he was ready to go on, every one of them the very picture of concentration.

'In that bubble under the sea, we could see all kinds of fish swimming around outside us as we were brought to one of the wise men of the city. We hadn't his language, of course, but he had ours, however he came by it, so we were able to ask him questions and answer his. One of the first things I asked him was how did they keep the sea out and themselves in.'

'"Oh," he said, "we have the books, the books of power."

'"D'you know," said I, "there's people back in our country too – that's Ireland, on the other side of the world – and they can do things like that. They're called druids and they have the books as well, and the power. But I never heard tell of any of them doing what ye have done here, building a city under the sea."'

At this, the men of the Fianna started whispering to each other, saying, 'Wouldn't it be mighty handy if we *had* a place like that, under a lake or what not, where we'd be able to hide from our enemies if all else failed us. Faith, we'll have to ask Taoscán Mac Liath about it. He might be able to build Tara again, under the River Boyne this time.'

Taoscán, of course, knew what they were saying, but his only reaction was a little smile to himself. He said nothing. Cormac it was who spoke: 'Silence at once! Let the story go on!'

Quietness fell, and the stranger described the type of houses, streets, and how the people got from one place to another.

'There were little trailers with two wheels,' he explained, 'and all the important people of the city travelled everywhere in them. Walking was not for them because they had tiny little feet on them, like the feet of young children, for all the world. Now, whether their feet were that way because they didn't walk, or they didn't walk much because their feet were that way, I don't know. I didn't like to enquire. They might think it bad manners. All I know is that they had the trailers to take them, and the money to pay the man, so walk they did not.'

He paused, but no one spoke. Fionn, out of courtesy, felt that he had to put in a word.

'There's only one thing more that I'd like to know about this wonderful land. Tell me, used they fight there?'

'No,' he replied firmly. 'There was no fighting because everyone was too much afraid.'

'Afraid! Afraid of what?' Fionn was getting interested in this new mystery. The thought crossed his mind that there might be lessons to be learned from the people of China which he could use when dealing with his enemies.

'Oh, they were frightened out of their wits of the fierce torture in that place.'

'Ahhh!' sighed Cormac. 'This is more like it. I was beginning to think that the people of that place had no bit of nature in them at all. Tell us about it! Did you see any of it?'

Every man was all an ear now. Here was something they could all be using if they knew how.

'I did. And I'll never forget it. It was the most wonderful thing you ever saw. And why? Because 'twas so simple. I was let in when they

were going over one of the enemies of the people
in the torture chamber. He was after doing some
desperate act of villainy and you can imagine
my shock when I was escorted to the lock-up
where he was and I heard this ferocious laughing
and screeching coming from inside. Of course,
I said to my guides, 'Tell me, is it a kind of feast
or something they're having in that house?'

'"Oh no," they said. "That's the prison, the place where all the evildoers are tortured."

'I hadn't a word to say to that, of course, but I said to myself, "That's a strange prison, to say they're all laughing inside." They took me in, anyway, very politely, and told me to look around to my heart's content – and I did. There were rows of big iron doors stretching down along the two sides of a long corridor, and so much laughing going on behind those doors that I began to wonder was I in my right mind at all. So, to put myself at ease I picked out a door where the laughing seemed louder than the rest, and knocked. Two men – and big burly men they were, the two of them as bald as that man there –' (pointing at Conán Maol) 'answered the door. I told them my business and they bowed and showed me in. There in front of me, in a dimly-lit cell, what should I see but a big table in the middle of the floor, with four leather straps on it, two at the top and two at the bottom. I had no trouble understanding what the straps were used for 'cos there on the table was a man, tied down solid, hand and foot.

'He stretched up his neck when he saw me and there was *terror* in his eyes! He shouted out something in a language I wasn't able to understand, but that was all he said 'cos the two big men went to work again. "Oh," I said to myself, "what kind of weapons do they use, now, I wonder. Is it red-hot irons, or what?"

'One of the big men went around the other side of the table, to give me a better view – fierce mannerly people, the Chinese – and when I saw him flexing his huge arms I thought he was surely going to grab the poor man on the table by the toes or by the neck or something and start twisting. Not a bit of it! He started humming to himself – and you could see the sweat rolling off of the poor man on the table – humming away as he turned and faced the wall.

''Twas only then I saw, on the wall, on a little shelf, a row of feathers – from the biggest swan feather on the left-hand side to the smallest wren's feather on the right. Man, when I saw him reaching along this shelf I thought he was gone off his head. Would you blame me! He walked up and down in front of the shelf and every few steps he'd stop and look at the man on the table, hum to himself, shake his head and walk on again – like he wouldn't be able to make up his mind about something – with a kind of sorrowful look on his face.

'I was just going to ask the second man what was wrong with him when he put up his hand into the middle of the feathers, gave a last look at the man tied down, and took out one of them. Very delicately he did it, too, for such a big man. You'd never think such thick fingers could handle so small a thing like a feather so neatly, but *he knew his trade!* But I will admit to every man here' (looking around at all his listeners, including King Cormac) 'that I thought I'd laugh at the sight of a monster of a man like that threatening another man with a feather! The fellow on the table wasn't laughing, though. Far from it! His voice was gone, and the sweat was in a pool under the table.

'The big man started down at the bottom of the table, at the soles of the poor man's feet, and started tickling him. Well, you'd hear his screeching a mile away. And by the time he got up to his oxters the breath was gone from him and he was gasping for mercy. He was nearly quenched from all the laughing! The other jailer, who was standing by my side looking on at all this, said, "That will do for now! Maybe our friend from the western world has seen enough."

'I nodded, of course – I was so surprised – and they released the poor man. Off he went, shaking, half-laughing, half-crying to himself. When I got control of my speech again I asked, "Is that the way ye deal with criminals and hoodoos in this place?"

'"That's it," they said. "And by the time that man is done once from head to toe he won't want to know anything about a second treatment. He's a model citizen for evermore! What other way could it be? Can you imagine if we started with the smallest feather and went up to the biggest, to the swan's tail feather! He'd be a raving lunatic by the time we finished!"'

The men of the Fianna were flabbergasted. They wanted to hear no more after that about the people, the houses or the streets, only, over and over again, about the feathers and how they were handled.

'Bless us and save us!' they babbled, 'and tell us – if we took you out now to the duck-house or the henhouse, could you pick out the feathers that he used?'

'Some of them, anyway. But you won't get all the feathers you need off one type of bird,' he said.

'Tomorrow is another day, and there's many a different kind of bird in this area. But come on! We'll settle for the ducks tonight ' – and there and then, Fionn took him out to the duck-house, a most unusual thing to do to a guest at a feast. But it was an important occasion, and in any case things could be done at the court of

Tara that might not be acceptable in other places. Torches were provided and the poor ducks got a quick plucking, not to mention the hens. A short time afterwards Fionn entered the hall again holding a mighty gabháil *(bundle)* of feathers, followed by the stranger and a group of the pluckers. Fionn landed the feathers on King Cormac's table and the stranger began to pick, choose and sort. Cormac sat stock still, more interested than if gold was being counted out in front of him, his two eyes riveted on the man's flying fingers.

'That one here, and this one there. . .' and on down the line until he came to the smallest feather, which the eye could hardly see – the nose-tickler, he called it, 'the one that'll drive a man out through himself with the laughing after, maybe, cudgels might have been hopping off of him for three days with no result.'

Then, when the sorting was done, 'There now,' said he. 'They're the ones we want. Gather round, everyone who wants to see, but breathe easy! One puff or cough and all my work is gone for nothing.'

The men thronged around, almost standing on each other's backs, every man ogling the feathers as if they were magic creatures.

Then, at a gesture from Cormac, they took

their seats again and the stranger spoke:

'I paid very careful attention in China to the different feathers for different jobs. There's one for the sole of the foot, one for behind the knee and one for the elbow, the palm of the hand, and for under the lug. In fact, there's no place that a feather can't be found for.'

'Hanam 'on diabhal! I can't wait to try them out for myself,' said Fionn. 'Hold on there, now!' and he picked out a feather, 'what's this one for?'

'That's the one for the top of the head,' the stranger said.

'Conán Maol! Stand up and come up here!' ordered Fionn. Conán rose, made his way to the high table, his bald head shining in the light of the torches.

'Sit down there, now, Conán, until I try this on you.'

He sat, and Fionn started. No effect.

'Am I doing it right?' Fionn asked the stranger, a disappointed look on his face.

'You are not. Watch me,' said the stranger, and then, for everyone to see, he gave a demonstration with the feather that left the men of the Fianna breathless with admiration – and Conán breathless from laughing. He was almost fit to collapse.

'Oh begob,' said Fionn, 'it works. It works! We must all get our own sets of these, we must!'

There was a mad heaving of men to their feet, scraping of chairs and a surge of excited voices. Every man in the hall was set to rush out, pluck what birds he could get his hands on, and make up a set of these wonderful weapons to try out on his worst enemies. Someone shouted, 'We'll start a war! 'Tis the only way!'

'None of that!' roared King Cormac in a dangerous voice, and all was silent again. But being a wise man he knew when to humour his men so he said, 'I'm looking for someone to do a small job for me this while, and it might involve a bit of persuasion' – and the words were hardly out of his mouth when a shower of hands was raised, all volunteers.

'Good men! I knew I could rely on the Fianna,' he smiled. 'Here, now, is what I want. There's a crowd of blackguards out there in Connemara and they owe me a lot of money – in overdue taxes. Ye could start with that crowd. If ye can make them pay me what I'm owed I'll make these feathers part of the standard equipment of the Fianna from now on.'

'We'll do it!' shouted Fionn. 'If there's any man that wants to stay at home, let him say so now,' and he looked around the hall.

Not a sound.

'I'm glad to hear that silence,' he laughed.

Fionn got the sorted set of feathers from the stranger and, the following day, when the other men had their sets sorted out, they started off for Connemara. They left their swords, spears and all other equipment behind them at Tara, and when the people saw them marching down the roads of Ireland with no weapons they said, 'Oh look! The Fianna must be going on holidays.'

But when they looked closer and saw each man wearing a row of feathers around his belt, short on one side, long on the other, like a lopsided dress, they said, 'Ah, here! The lads are gone like Indians. There's something wrong!'

After a day's steady marching they arrived at the dún of Ó Flátharta, chief of the blackguards – Ó Flátharta Gorm, as he was called, because he used to wear blue war-paint to terrify his enemies. Fionn stepped up to the gate of the dún, near Indreabhán, and called out, 'Open the gate! We have a small bit of talking to do. A message from King Cormac, High King of all Ireland, including Indreabhán!'

The gate was opened and when Ó Flátharta saw that they had no weapons he said in his most friendly voice, 'Come in, come in! And tell me what brings ye to this part of Ireland. My! My! Isn't it lovely decorations ye're wearing, ladies – lads, I mean!'

He was highly amused when he saw the feathers. Fionn knew well when he was being insulted, so he said in a very deliberate voice, 'Uasal Ó Flátharta, the message from King Cormac is that you owe him money, and if you're not inclined to pay we have orders to – ah! – make a withdrawal from your treasury. . . with or without the key.'

'Hu-hu-huu!' cackled Ó Flátharta. 'My treasury, is it, ladies?'

There was a rustle of movement among the men behind Fionn, but he held up his hand for restraint. Ó Flátharta spoke on, poison coming into his voice now, 'You have no weapons, Fionn Mac Cumhail, and there isn't a man walking that I respect without a sword in his hand. I'll pay no man until he makes me do it. Tell that to your King Cormac.'

'I'd think a small bit more about it, if I were you,' said Fionn in his Sunday voice. 'We're peaceful men, but if we're rubbed the wrong way. . . If your druid isn't able to tell you stories about what we do to men like you, you should give him his walking papers and get a man that's more up with the times. You'll last longer as chief that way! So look! Why wouldn't you deliver King Cormac's taxes into our safe hands now, like a good man, and there'll be no more noise.'

Ó Flátharta wouldn't hear of it. He said he'd ram them all into his deepest dungeon and pour boiling gruel in on top of them if they didn't clear off back to Tara, and be quick about it.

'All right,' said Fionn mildly. 'But you'll meet us again. . . shortly!'

'Ye'll be welcome as far as the gate here. And bring your grandmother with you the next time. Heee! Haaaww! Hawww!'

They left, and Ó Flátharta's men conveyed them for five miles of the road, mocking them. In the dún of Indreabhán that night there was a great celebration. The Fianna defeated and humiliated without a blow struck! All Cormac's gold safe in Connemara! Why wouldn't they celebrate! *Even the sentries joined in the merrymaking.*

But when they were at their jolliest in the feasting-hall of Indreabhán the Fianna returned and went about their business in their usual silent, deadly way. They padded through the darkness around the unguarded dún and soon found the window of Ó Flátharta's sleeping-

31

chamber. Silently, with the hands of trained men, they made the window into a door, went in, repaired the wall after them, and listened. No sound. Ó Flátharta was too busy feasting and laughing with all his men, giving orders to his poets and his harpers to compose music and words about the defeat of the cowardly Fianna.

If only he knew!

Fionn and the men settled themselves comfortably in the chief's quarters and waited for the feast to take its course, fingering the feathers all the time, laughing in the darkness at the thought of the fun to come.

Well into the small hours of the morning a step was heard in the corridor, then a voice at the door, humming a happy little tune. Ó Flátharta threw open the door and tottered in, his servant a step behind him. He turned and said to the boy, 'That will be all! Take your rest, boy, and call me the day after tomorrow, 'cos I'm jaded.'

He shut and barred the door, as was his usual custom at night, yawning and talking to himself all the while, then collapsed into bed and was snoring before his head hit the pillow. But the third snore had hardly passed his lips when a hairy hand sailed out of the darkness and clamped itself over his mouth.

'Gnhhh! Uhhh!' Drunk and tired as he was Ó Flátharta struggled furiously.

'Shhh!' warned Fionn, smiling down at him. There was silence. Diarmaid lit a candle and set it on a little table beside the bed where Ó Flátharta kept his false teeth at night. The chief's eyes darted around the room, saw all the men dotted here and there, and he thought his last hour had surely come. But he could do nothing because Fionn's hand was still over his mouth and his other fist was held over his head, like a boulder ready to fall.

Fionn nodded to the men and four of them moved to the bed. Two sat on Ó Flátharta's legs, two on his hands, and the night's work began. Keeping one hand over the chief's mouth Fionn picked the toe-feather out of his belt, very deliberately, too, so that the man on the bed could get the full benefit of seeing him. Ó Flátharta's eyes followed his every move, expecting a knife, no doubt.

Fionn held up the feather.

'I suppose you thought this was a decoration. Well, you'll soon see!' He started, and under his hand Ó Flátharta started too –

'Uu-huu-huuuu! Mmmm-mmmm!'

Fionn turned to Conán.

'Conán! Here! Keep your hand on his face

here, and I'll have my two hands to work with.'

That was done and he started in earnest, beginning below at the toes and working up, changing feathers every so often. He enjoyed himself so much that he nearly wore out his fine set of feathers. And Conán was able to take away his hand from Ó Flátharta's mouth after a short while because that man was too weak from laughing to stir. In fact Fionn said, ''Tis *better* to take off your hand, Conán, 'cos when the crowd outside hear him – *if* they hear him – they won't know in the name of Crom what's going on.'

By this time an excited crowd of Ó Flátharta's

men had gathered in the corridor outside, wondering what was happening in the room, and what should they do. By now Fionn had got to the sensitive spot behind Ó Flátharta's knee and the real merriment started. The chief roared and bellowed and screamed for mercy – a sure sign that he was a money-grabber, and well Fionn knew it because Taoscán Mac Liath had told him, 'The man who loves money, tickle behind the knee and he'll go mad.'

Fionn was getting so much fun out of it that he wore out the knee-feather – couldn't resist it. But Diarmaid saw the danger, and saw that Fionn did not: Ó Flátharta was gone black in the face from lack of breath.

'Here! Here! Stop, Fionn! He'll get a heart-attack. He's no good to us dead.'

Fionn stopped. He took a rest for a minute and listened. By now the guards in the corridor were worried men.

'Hi! Chief, chief! Are you all right?'

The answer they got left them no wiser. All he could say was 'Eeee-aaa-ah-ah-ahh!' because Fionn was working again. They thought there must surely be evil spirits in the room with him. Yet they dared not break down the door for fear of the anger of Ó Flátharta.

By the time Fionn had finished his victim's

breath was gone for good and he was nearly a gibbering maniac.

'I think 'tis time we had an audience for my handiwork,' said Fionn, striding across and throwing off the bar from the door. The guards saw their chance, rushed in with weapons drawn, but when they saw who was there they hesitated.

'Softly now, men of Indreabhán,' said Fionn with mockery in his voice.

'Is it the custom in these parts to attack men with no weapons?'

That stopped them. And while they were standing still they had time to think better of what it was that they were about to do. To attack Fionn Mac Cumhail was a dangerous business at the best of times, but to do so in a narrow, darkened room would be the work of a man intent on committing suicide. So no one moved.

'What has your chief to say?' Fionn asked them quietly.

The guards looked at Ó Flátharta, who was just beginning to come back to himself. He was cringing in a corner of the bed, shaking, eating his fingers and whispering frightfully to himself in a strange language. They thought he must have come straight out of the Black House of Féitheacha Daoil, a thought to make any man's blood turn to water.

'What devil's work did ye do to him?' whispered the guards. 'What spell did ye put on our beloved chief?'

'Look, now! We didn't lay a weapon or a rough hand on him,' said Fionn.

'He's bewitched, so,' they said.

'No,' thundered Fionn. 'That man was defeated with this' – holding up a feather. They all gaped. Fionn took two steps towards them and they ran, trampling each other in their haste to escape. They were completely confused now and had lost all heart for fighting. And the one question that tormented every man's brain was, 'How could the mighty Ó Flátharta Gorm be defeated by a feather?'

But they knew Fionn would not lie – men might call him many ugly things, but no man in any of the four corners of Ireland could call him a liar. So they gathered in the courtyard of the dún and went into a huddle, frightened men, every one of them.

After a few minutes Fionn strolled out, followed by the other men of the Fianna, and only now did the guards notice that every man was wearing feathers around his waist, all arranged according to size. So they began to edge back into a corner shouting, 'Fionn Mac Cumhail, don't come any nearer to us! You're a dangerous devil, and we're afraid of you!'

They threw their eyes up the wall, looking for a way out, but before anyone could stir a scraping sound was heard from the direction of Ó Flátharta's chamber and out crept the man himself, out along the wall.

'Men,' said he, sobbing, 'get my money-chest! Get it, quick. Ye know where it is!'

Three of his guards sprinted out of their corner and ran for the chest, glad of an excuse to escape.

'Take it all,' whimpered Ó Flátharta to Fionn, 'take it all! Look! I'll pay ten years' tax now in advance. Only go away and take your cursed feathers with you.'

They went, thanking him politely, and no man interfered with them this time, or conveyed them on their way.

Ó Flátharta would not reveal to his men what Fionn had done to him, but the following day he went out alone and killed every bird in the dún, all the hens, ducks, geese, even goslings; anything with two legs and feathers met a quick end. And ever afterwards, as long as he lived, no bird, tame or wild, was safe near the dún of Indreabhán.

Naturally, rumours spread through the land

of Ireland and people began to put two and two together and come to all sorts of conclusions. But most people agreed that there was something strange about the feathers carried by the Fianna, even if that something was not known for sure. No one was prepared to risk finding out, so from that time on, let them only appear in a place without weapons, but wearing the feathers, and a sudden end was guaranteed to whatever trouble or disturbance called them there in the first place.

And as a result of men not knowing what was in store for them if they acted the ruffian there was a huge improvement in people's conduct in the kingdom of the ard-rí *(high king)*, Cormac, which proves that the old saying is true:

'The devil you don't know is worse than the one you do.'

King Cormac's
Fighting Academy

There was one particular year in Tara and times *were* bad. King Cormac watched day after day as Fionn and the men of the Fianna wandered around with their hands in their pockets, or playing pitch and toss, they had so little to do. Even in the feasting hall they sat miserably, drumming their fingers on the tables out of sheer boredom. For at last the kings of Ireland had got the message, after many defeats, that it was no good fighting the Fianna.

'Only wasting our energy,' they said. 'They always beat us. We'll give it up entirely and do what Conor O'Connor did – start a síbín or a lodging-house. There'd be more of a future in it.'

That was all very fine for them, but what about the Fianna, trained men whose only purpose in life was fighting and who knew no other job?

King Cormac was a worried man so he called the Fianna together.

'Look here,' he announced. 'I can't have my army idling away the time around here, getting fat and lazy. You're only bursting your trousers from all the eating you're doing! Work will have to be found, Fionn.'

'I couldn't agree more, your highness,' sighed Fionn.

So a meeting was called with Cormac, Fionn and the royal druid, Taoscán Mac Liath, present and they adjourned to the royal thinking-chamber to see whether they could put matters straight.

'I want ideas,' growled Cormac, 'and I want them fast.'

'We'll do our best, never fear, your highness,' beamed Fionn.

They *did* their best, long and hard, scratching their heads and rubbing their chins, but no ideas were coming. At last Cormac got up, banged the table and shouted, 'You're all red useless! Taoscán, I'm surprised at you! I'm paying Fionn to do the fighting so I don't mind him not having ideas, but you! You're supposed to be a thinking man!'

'Oh leave me alone, leave me alone,' moaned Taoscán. 'My head is addled this last week. A new recipe I'm trying to get for the cupóg (*dock-leaf*) wine, and d'you know what? I'm not in the better of it. I'm not thinking straight at all. Have you any ideas yourself, King Cormac?'

'What I need is gold! Gold! And an amount of it! I'm bankrupt otherwise.'

'Well, as far as I know there's only two ways of getting gold,' said Fionn, pulling himself up. 'You steal it or you work for it – some kind of business or other.'

'Hah? Sure, I can't steal it! I'm supposed to be the law in this misfortunate land and you my trusted captain. We can hardly go around robbing people – not without a good excuse, anyway – and there's no wars going on at the moment.'

'There's only one thing left, so', said Fionn hopefully. 'We'll have to start up some kind of a business.'

Cormac's face changed colour. He ground his teeth, shouted, 'Business! A business for the ard-rí *(high king)* of Ireland? Is it trying to make a tradesman out of me you are? How dare you, Fionn Mac Cumhail!'

Fionn knew from long experience that when Cormac used his full name he was very displeased indeed, so he changed his tone and in his silkiest voice of plámás *(flattery)* replied, 'Nooo! No, no! Don't take me up wrong, now. Aren't we, the men of the Fianna, here!'

'Blast ye, 'tis well I know it,' snorted Cormac. 'Haven't ye me eaten out of house and home, ye hungry crowd of savages.'

'Please, your highness, don't get personal, now. I'm only saying. . .' – pointing modestly at himself – 'wouldn't *we* make a great business for you.'

'How do you mean?' muttered Cormac after a small silence. Even Taoscán was pricking up his ears now and showing interest.

'Well, you see. . . we all know there's no wars going on these times. And as you say, your highness, we're only getting fat and lazy from mooching around. So, wouldn't it be the height of good sense if messengers were sent in your name to the four corners of the known world to announce to all the kings there that there's great training to be got here in Tara for their armies, if they want to send them along to us. We'll give them the benefit of our experience. And the beauty of it is, we'll be keeping our-selves in training as well.'

'Begor!' Cormac muttered in a distant voice, looking at the table all the while. He was half stunned to get any such clever suggestion from Fionn. At last he got up.

'Faith, Fionn, that isn't the worst idea you ever had!' and a smile broke out on his face.

Visions of gold and kings from the ends of the world coming to his house fluttered across his mind, and the next words he spoke were, 'We'll get my scribe, Mac Cleite, to write out a bundle of notices immediately and I'll send them off this day.'

That was done, and at that same hour he gave orders that Tara was to be whitewashed from the ground up, and down again, in preparation for the guests. That was done also and it kept the men of the Fianna occupied for a time, but a day came at last when no more could be done. The brushes were put away and everyone settled himself to wait for the customers to arrive.

They waited one week. And another. And another. The summer wore on, but no strangers showed themselves on the long straight road up to Tara, no matter how hard King Cormac stared at it from the top of the walls. His spirits began to sink again.

'It looks very like no one is going to come. Blast it, but did the messengers ever deliver their messages at all?'

He called them, every one, and ordered them to repeat their stories again – 'Did you leave my message with the King of France? With the King of Spain? With King Arthur?'

'Of course we did, your highness. And they

all promised they'd take up your kind offer as soon as 'twas convenient.'

'Oh, the lying thieves,' shouted Cormac. 'They never meant a word of it! I'm the only king in the whole world left with any bit of kindness or truth in him.'

'You are! You are!' They all agreed, nodding their heads wisely. But then one of the messengers spoke up.

'I don't know, now. The King of France, he seemed fierce interested. He said, though, that he was having deadly trouble with his son, and that it wouldn't be easy for him to send anyone until he'd have that bit of bother put by him. He needs every man he can get.'

'Ah, what kind of a king is he if he can't keep smacht (obedience) on his own son!' mouthed Cormac. 'Sure, if he thought about it wouldn't he do far better to get his men properly trained here. Then he'd need only half the army he needs now.'

That conversation fell by the wayside, and a hundred more like it, and they were still there a week later twiddling their thumbs when a cloud of dust was noticed on the horizon.

'Huh! At least someone is keeping the grass from the road,' said Fionn. He turned to Cormac. 'Will I go to the butt of the hill and see who it is?'

'You might as well,' said Cormac.

Fionn went down, at his ease, but half excited of course, wondering whether it might be their first customer. He planted himself in the middle of the road, leaned on his spear, and waited. A short time later a group of men rode up to him. Fionn stood his ground and when they clattered up close he noticed that their leader was a large man, with very much the appearance of a king about him. And if more proof was needed, a gold crown was perched at an angle on his head. Fionn straightened up, getting himself ready to look respectful if he needed to, but also keeping his ears cocked to hear what they were saying, in case he might be able to place them by their language. He *did* recognise it as soon as they spoke. They were talking none other than French, and a fine body of men they were, too. Any leader might be proud to ride in front of them.

'Fighting men, all,' thought Fionn, looking them over shrewdly. No better man than he to recognise his own type.

'Good morrow, men. Are ye going to Tara, by any chance?'

'Oui *(Yes)*,' replied the leader.

'Aha! Do I hear the voice of a man of France?

I was in that country not so long ago at all, and I enjoyed myself no end.'

"Oo are you, m'sieur?' asked the leader, smiling a little smile, as if he were speaking to a young child.

'Me? I'm Fionn Mac Cumhail.'

The leader's face changed.

'Aha! Ze very man we come to see! I believe you have trouble with my parent once, no?'

'Not at all!' said Fionn heartily. 'A small misunderstanding only. We settled that up before I left and there was no more about it. But, anyway, who might you be, if you don't mind me asking?'

'I am Pipin, son of zat king. I come to meet zis great warrior, Finn Ma' Kool, and now I meet him. Excellent! Zese here, zey are my men and we wish to learn ze tricks of ze trade. My parent, he say zat you are fierce fighter, zat you have all ze dirty tricks. Mon dieu (my God), his admiration when you drive ze royal armee into La Manche! Still zey are fishing zem out. Magnifique!'

'Begor, 'tis well I remember it,' and Fionn smiled into his beard. 'Ah, 'tisn't often you'd come across good clean fun the like of that anymore. But look, King Cormac is impatient to meet you. Come on up to Tara and I'll bring you to him. Ye can settle up about the training and the fees between ye.'

They went up. Cormac was out at the gate waiting for them.

'Well, well, well! Who have we here, Fionn?'

'Prince Pipin, son of the King of France. He's here to learn how to fight right.'

'Indeed he came to the right spot,' cackled Cormac. 'We'll teach ye, all right.'

Pipin and his men – thirty in all – dismounted and were shown into the hall of Tara. Friendly men they seemed, too, looking here and there about them, passing comments to each other every time they noticed something unusual. All in all, they were very impressed with Tara, as indeed they should be since the place gleamed white from top to bottom.

While his men were being shown the country around Tara, Prince Pipin was in deep discussion with Cormac, Fionn and Taoscán Mac Liath, working out the details of the training – type, length and price. A hard session of bargaining it was, but when all was arranged to everyone's satisfaction Pipin asked, 'When may I look on ze Fianna in action?'

'Oh, we can arrange a nice handy little tournament any time ye like,' said Cormac, 'a friendly challenge, to see how good ye are, you

know. Before we can teach ye we have to see how much ye know.'

'But of course!' cried Pipin.

Cormac clapped his hands. A servant entered. 'Tell the men to be ready in a half hour. Our visitor must be kept happy at all costs, heh.'

The Fianna needed no more telling. Thirty minutes later they were lined up in the yard, their equipment gleaming in the sunlight, the glitter of hard polishing every day since the whitewashing of Tara had ended. They straightened themselves to their full height, thirty of them, all ready to engage the men of France in any game of their choosing. But first Cormac stood out and announced to all, 'This isn't to be any way bad-tempered. A bit of fun now, mind. And just in case tempers *might* get out of order ye're only allowed to use sticks. No weapons!'

The two rows of men faced each other and at a signal from Fionn they began to fight man to man. Their meeting was short and sharp – too sharp for the men of France, because in a few minutes they lay flat on their backs, while the Fianna stood leaning on their staffs, smiling down at them. Prince Pipin stood, his two eyes out on stalks with wonder.

'Eez clear now why my parent could not forget ze land of Ireland! Such fighters!'

Fionn was picking his nails modestly.

'They're good, aren't they?' he said.

'Sacre bleu (*sacred blue*), zey are superb! Teach my men to fight like zat and I reward you much.'

'Heh – hee!' chuckled Cormac to himself. 'Just what I wanted to hear.'

Money-bags jingled sweetly in his mind as he rubbed his hands together with delight under his cloak.

The serious business of training the men of France began that very day and it continued, hour after hour, for four solid weeks. With every day that passed the Fianna were finding it harder to better the Frenchmen. At the end of two weeks they were out of breath by the time they won; at the end of three weeks they snatched victory only by the breadth of their nails, and at the end of four weeks they had to call it quits without winning – a dead heat. At that point Fionn called Cormac aside and whispered to him urgently. Cormac nodded and held up his hands for silence.

'Men of France, I'm delighted to be able to announce that your training is at an end. There's very little more to be learnt here.'

The Frenchmen's reply was a growl of disappointment because for the first time they were beginning to enjoy themselves fully and to realise that given another few days they might teach their teachers a thing or two. Prince Pipin thought so too, but he kept his feelings to himself and said instead, 'Wondrous! Perfection! Come, we settle our debts now, eh?'

'No hurry, no hurry!' replied Cormac, but it was obvious that he was anxious to see the gold.

That night a farewell feast was held and during

the course of the meal Pipin sent for his money chest. It was placed in a position of honour before King Cormac and, naturally, every man's eyes were on it. After all their weeks' work they were anxious to see the reward. Carefully Pipin took a golden key from round his neck, unlocked the chest and threw back the lid. There, dazzling the eyes of all, was a heap of bright gold, enough to make every man's mouth water. Pipin let them drink in the glow of it for a little time, laughing and joking all the while with Cormac. Then suddenly he snapped down the lid, turned the key, gave it to Cormac saying, 'Zere you are. All yours.'

Cormac, in front of all his men, had to show manners, so he pretended that he didn't care much for the gold anyway and pushed the chest to one side of the table. Then two claps of his hands brought the servants with double servings of poitín and men sighed with contentment. A song was called for from the bard, and there was silence.

Everything was going as it should, but if the men of the Fianna had not been so busy enjoying the food and drink they might have noticed that for every goblet of poitín they drank the Frenchmen swallowed only a small mouthful. They talked, indeed, and laughed and joked, but there

54

was something on their minds, especially on Pipin's mind. He kept a tight eye on the chest and made sure that none of the servants, or anyone else either, attempted to move it. Indeed, no one did, for, as the feast wore on the noise got louder, the talk sillier and the sound of men hitting the flags of the floor more noticeable – and they weren't Frenchmen, either.

In the small hours Fionn fell asleep on the table and even Cormac had to be carried out on the royal stretcher looking sadly the worse for wear.

When the last of the Fianna were either on the tables or under them, and the hall of Tara was like a sawmill from the sounds of snoring, Prince Pipin rose up and said, 'So! All of zese pigs are now in ze land of dreams. Remember our plan, my men,' and at that every one of the men of France set about cutting a big sheaf of hair out of the beard of every sleeping man, including Taoscán Mac Liath. No doubt King Cormac would have got the same treatment except for his exit on the royal stretcher, lucky man.

At a signal from Pipin his men filed out, every man with a fistful of hair of different colours, and two men bringing up the rear carrying the chest. Down the straight road from Tara they went, to where their ships were waiting. By the time any of the Fianna opened an eye the following day – very far out in the day, too, – they were well over the horizon on their way to France with Prince Pipin humming a happy little song to himself in the prow of the ship.

Fionn was the first to stir, when a sunbeam from high in the noon sky poked its way into his face. He snorted, moved his arms up on the table where he was lying, made an attempt to turn around – in his bed, as he thought – to find a more comfortable position, and. . . fell with a crash on the floor and rolled under the table. He woke with a shout, thinking that he was attacked, and tried to jump up.

CRACK!!!

His head thudded against the solid beams of the table. He was convinced now!

'Get off of me, ye cowardly villains!' he bellowed, standing up and sending the table flying – down on top of other men still in the land of dreams. They, in their turn, let out fearsome shrieks, thinking they were being attacked and calling for blood.

Oh, to try to describe the confusion in the hall of Tara that morning! It was bad enough to wake King Cormac – and he was no light sleeper on a morning after a feast. He came down, holding his head in his two hands, looked at the state of the hall, and nearly left himself with the fit of temper that came over him.

'In the name of the twisted –' and he was just about to launch an attack of abuse that would rise blisters on them when he stopped. He looked oddly at Fionn.

'What happened to your face, Fionn?'

'My face?'

'And yours, Diarmaid, and Goll's – in fact, everyone's,' looking from one to the other.

Only then, when they looked at each other, did they realise what the men of France had done. Every man's hands fumbled for his own face and each face lit up red with the dishonour that had been done. But every man, when he found out that the same had been done to Taoscán Mac Liath, druid to the high king of Ireland, was scandalised entirely, and forgot his own missing hairs.

'What kind of a crowd of savages are they, them men of France?'

'Have they any bit of religion in them at all? A dirty deed like that!'

'Have they any bit of *sense*, you mean! Surely they don't think we'll leave that go with them.'

The only one not to speak was Taoscán. But he had no need to. His face did all the talking that was necessary. No man there could ever remember seeing him so angry. He went off, silently, deadly, and shut the door of his cave on himself without a word to anyone.

'I wouldn't like to be in France tonight,' muttered King Cormac to himself.

They parted then, each man to his own mirror to try to repair the damage as best he could. No one thought about, or even noticed, that the chest of gold was gone. Even if they had it would have been the last thing on their minds at a time like this.

By this time Prince Pipin and this thirty men were on the high road to Paris and the court of the king, throwing smiles and salutes at the people of France on all sides. Long before they came to the palace the news of their coming arrived before them and the king was out, happy to welcome them home, He questioned them: Were they made welcome at Tara? What was the training like? Would they recommend the place? and other questions of a like nature. To every question he asked he got an answer that pleased him – until the question of money arose. Prince Pipin could hardly hold in the laughter as he told his father how he had tricked the gobdaws *(fools)* of Ireland: 'And look, my father,' he cried, holding up a fist of hair, 'look!

In our hands, back we have brought a gift for you and for mamma with which to stuff ze cushions!'

He saw that his father had no clue of what he was talking about, so he explained the cutting off of the beards. As he talked he warmed to his story, shaking with laughter at this fine trick, all his men joining in, getting merrier and merrier. But one man was not enjoying the joke. And that man was the king. Just as Pipin was getting to the funniest part of the story, the tears flowing down his face with mirth, he was stopped in his tracks by a roar of rage from his father: 'Silence, fool!'

Pipin's jaw kept wagging for a few seconds but his talk stopped. In the silence he stared at his father while he tried to straighten his face. The king was glaring at his men.

'So! Ze honour of France is to be dragged through ze filth by ze royal son and his trusted men! Never have I heard such a despicable trick' – and his voice put poison into the word.

'I have a mind to—' but before he could go on his druid, who was standing at his shoulder, sent up a shriek, rushed forward, snatched a bunch of hair from the hand of one of the dumbfounded men and began to sort through it in a frenzy.

'I recognise it! I recognise it!' he moaned to the king. 'Zis 'air belongs to Taoscán Mac Liath, druid to the high king himself. It will be terrible for us now. I know! Terrible!'

'Please to explain!' cried the king.

The druid did so, and the clearer the truth became, the paler the king became. He turned to Pipin.

'Impudent idiot! Dumbhead! You – yes, you – will pay for zis evil deed! Back you will go, on ze knees, and beg, grovel in ze gravel for merci!'

At these harsh words from his father Pipin's speech came back very quickly, and hard words he had for the king in return. He called the older man what no son should call a father and then rushed out, followed by his men, mounted his horse and was off before he could be stopped.

Little did the king know it, but it was his luck that they were gone from Paris for from that day on, everywhere they went they were followed by plagues of rats, bats, snakes and spiders, fogs from the air and evil noises from the ground. At last they became a hunted little band, showing their faces in town or village only at the risk of being hunted away by the people with sticks, stones and cowdung. They were reduced to the level of wandering beggars, a sad come-down, surely, for the son of the king and his men.

But every man, even the stupidest, or the proudest, comes to his senses at last under enough misfortune, and Pipin was no exception. A day dawned when his men, loyal though they were, would take no more.

'Enough of zis, Pipin,' they said. 'We will have to face for Ireland, like eet or not.'

'First we must face my father, ze king,' replied Pipin mournfully, and that was what they did.

Fathers being forgiving people, the king forgave Pipin for all the trouble he had brought on the kingdom. But he had this to say too: 'Me to forgive you ees all very fine, but no end will there be to ze misfortunes zat are on you 'till ze forgiveness is had from ze man you have insulted most of all, Taoscán Mac Liath.'

The thought of it alone filled Pipin with the horrors, but try as he might he could think of no way out of it. So to Ireland and to Tara he went.

* * * * *

Taoscán Mac Liath was not a revengeful man, but a vile deed had been done and the full price

must be paid, so Pipin was left begging outside the gates of Tara – in his bare feet, too – for eight days and nights, while men came and went about their business, taking no more notice of him than if he were a stray dog. Indeed, if he was a stray dog a lot more notice *would* have been taken of him. His pride was stung to its very roots by this hard treatment but he persevered until, on the morning of the ninth day, a summons was sent to him from King Cormac, 'to attend his highness' pleasure, at once!'

He jumped to it, of course. Hard to blame him for that!

Bundled into Cormac's audience chamber, pushed to his knees, he was kept there in suspense while Fionn, Taoscán and Cormac talked among themselves, throwing severe glances in his direction every so often.

'Turn him into a mushroom!' pleaded Fionn with Taoscán.

'No! A ciaróg *(beetle)*!' ordered Cormac, with a poisonous glare at Pipin.

The poor prince cringed miserably on the cold flagstones, hearing only snatches of their conversation but guessing that they meant no good to him.

'All right, so,' hissed Fionn, with another menacing look at Pipin. 'We'll put him in dungeon number seven, and half-fill it with water. But I still think we're letting him off too soft. Couldn't we boil the water at least?'

Taoscán looked at Pipin, and the spectacle of him, a king's son, kneeling terrified in a strange land, brought to his mind a picture of a small boy long ago, lost in a wild, rocky valley of Kerry, crying pitifully as night and the creatures of the night closed in and the laughing face and fuzzy whiskers and strong arms of the man who had lifted him high and warm above the clutching darkness. His anger vanished, even as his fingers curled around the place where his beard had once grown long and smooth.

'No,' he said, his eyes vague and misty in the bright room. 'No. A servant is what I need. A good servant. And this is the one.'

'What?' King Cormac and Fionn gaped at each other.

'Are you all right?' asked Cormac urgently. 'D'you want to sit down for a minute?'

Taoscán shook himself and straightened up. 'He'll be my servant for a year and a day. That'd be the best for all of us.'

'Stop! Wait! Hold on a minute, now!' cried Fionn. 'There's no sense in this. Every villain from foreign parts will think he can come here and shave us when he likes if we do what you're saying here!'

'My servant he'll be, for a year and a day,' repeated Taoscán in a low voice of authority.

'Make it seven years and a day, at least, can't you?' But Taoscán was gone, out the door, beckoning Pipin to follow him.

*   *   *   *   *

Exactly a year and a day later Pipin, prince of France, turned his back for the last time on Tara and set out for his father's court. What a change was there! The dishonourable trickster of the year before was now a man who could take his place in any company. Under the sure guidance of Taoscán he had become willing, trusted, friendly and well-liked.

He went back to his father, who was amazed at the change in him for the better. He was so amazed that he resigned his throne to him a short while afterwards and took a long holiday in this land of Ireland where such miracles could be worked. He hunted, feasted, danced and laughed with the men of the Fianna and enjoyed himself so much that no year afterwards, for as long as he lived, did he neglect to spend some time there.

And Prince Pipin – now King Pipin – ruled

wisely and justly in France and remained a friend to Ireland all his days – a fool made wise, an enemy made a friend, by the patience of Taoscán Mac Liath.

Fionn and the Mermaids

When Fionn's son, Oisín, was young and in his cradle he was like no ordinary child. Even at the age of nine months he was huge, so much so that Fionn and his wife had their hands full in trying to feed him. They couldn't keep him supplied with milk even though they had four of the finest Kerry cows in their yard. He drank a barrel of milk every day, as much as they could produce, and left nothing for Fionn to drink for his dinner. This went on for a time, but then the cows began to fail and Fionn decided to call a halt.

'We'll have to stop this,' he pounded one day. 'That fellow, he'll break us! There's only one thing for it: we'll have to drown him, or else get him off the milk and on to some cheaper food.'

His wife wouldn't hear of drowning Oisín, so there was nothing for it but to change his feeding-habits.

Fionn considered.

'D'you know,' he said to his wife, 'the last

time I was in Eamhain Macha I heard a rumour that fish is grand food altogether for old people 'cos 'tis easy on the stomach. And if 'tis easy on old people, surely 'twould be just as good for a young lad! I'll go down to the sea to-morrow when I have a fishing-rod made up and I'll see can I catch anything to feed ould hungry-guts there.'

That evening he went into the wood of Allen, cut down the straightest stick he could find, trimmed the small branches from it and brought it home. He went to the hole in the thatch, reached in and pulled out the ball of catgut which he had stored there for this and other such emergencies. At last the rod was ready, all except the hook. But that was no problem to Fionn. He knew the very place where such an item was to be got, and he slept the sleep of the just that night.

Early next morning he was prowling around the house – much earlier than either his wife or Oisín – excited at the thought of his brilliant plan. He crept to Oisín's cradle, peered in. The child was sound asleep. Carefully, his great hairy fingers unclasped the wolf's tooth that tied the napkin, removed it gently, while all the time Oisín slept peacefully. This delicate job completed, he tiptoed out of the house and began his journey to the seaside. Later, when his wife was wakened by Oisín's roaring and discovered the theft there was war in the house, but Fionn was well on his road and beyond caring then.

The sun shone merrily down on this beautiful morning as Fionn strode on his way, whistling and admiring the greenness of the countryside. So happy did he feel that even when he was passing Geata na Spioraid, the notorious haunted spot on the road, no shadow of anxiety crossed his mind. It was a place with an ugly reputation, partly due to its gloominess because of the tall trees which grew there to the very edges of the road. But even if Fionn had been thinking of all this it would have caused him no worry. He was afraid of nothing, either in the dark of the night or the broad light of noon. He had almost passed the gloom of the trees when there, before him in the road as if out of thin air, crouched a dark motionless figure bent over a blackthorn stick. He jerked to a stop, the rod clattering to the ground.

'By the silver hand of Nuada!' he breathed. 'Who are you?'

Now the lips were moving and a wheezing voice quivered. 'Fionn Mac Cumhail, is it to the Black Cliff you're going this day?'

He ignored the question, his mind trying to

grasp how this woman – for he had decided that the voice was a woman's – could know his name.

She was speaking again, the eyes fixed on him always. 'You can tell me if you like, but I know anyway. 'Tis to the Black Cliff and the Dark Pool you're going.' Then the voice changed, light and airy. 'You're right, too. That's the place you'll catch the fish to feed your son.'

Fionn could keep silent no longer.

'You're the surprising woman, surely. Tell me, how do you know so much about me?'

'That I can't tell you, but there's something I can! What kind of fish are you trying to catch?'

A blush spread over Fionn's neck. He had no idea. One type of fish was the same to him as another, but how could he admit that? If he were asked about rabbits, deer or birds he could answer in any kind of detail, but fish! He had no clue. The old woman knew it, too. A twisted smile flitted across her lips and she twittered.

'Take my word for it, what you want is shark-meat. Remember that! Shark! That's the stuff to put his hair growing.'

'Shark? Faith, I'll think of that. Is it nice to eat?'

'You'd lick your fingers after it. But the only bother is to catch them. They're a small bit on the wicked side. But, sure, no bother to a big beater of a fellow like yourself.'

Again the little smile chased itself across her yellow face, but Fionn noticed nothing; this time she was looking at her stick, not at him.

'Go to the black pool under the cliff,' she rattled suddenly, startling Fionn. 'Throw in your hook there and you'll catch something. What kind of bait have you?'

'Bait?' slobbered Fionn blankly.

'Yes, bait!' she snapped. 'You don't expect to catch fish with a bare hook, do you?'

'I'm beat, so. Sure, I never thought of that. I was in such a hurry out of the house for fear my wife'd notice the pin gone that I forgot to dig worms. But' – brightening suddenly – 'couldn't I pull down a bit of the cliff? There's bound to be worms there someplace.'

'What kind of fisherman are you?' sneered the yellow face. 'Do you think sharks have no respect for themselves, that they'd take fresh worms like them? You might catch a conger eel or a mullet but that's the best you'd do.'

If truth were told Fionn would get equal pleasure from eating shark, eels or mullet, heads and tails, without enquiring too closely which was which, but to admit as much would, he felt, be to his great dishonour so he made no interruption as she continued.

'Here now is something I'll give you to put on your hook, and then you'll catch fish,' and she turned from him to take something from a small black bag strung about her neck, something wrapped in a piece of catskin.

'Here! Keep that in a safe place until you're ready to start and I'll guarantee you won't come home empty-handed this day.'

Fionn fingered it, then put it carefully in his pouch.

'Thank you kindly, ma'am. And I won't forget you if I have a bit to spare.'

He glanced at the sky, at the sun rising towards its mid-course.

'I'd better be going now, before the day is gone and I'd have nothing to show for my travels,' but already she was tottering away, muttering to herself among the trees.

He hurried on, considering in his mind whether he should use the thing she had given him as a bait, and in what seemed a short time he found himself at the top of a cliff, looking down.

'Hanam 'on diabhal, isn't that the evil-looking place, down there,' he muttered, gazing at the stretch of water at the foot of the cliff. Even though it was the middle of the noon day he could see no trace of the bottom through the dark water.

'I'd want to keep well back from the edge of this place,' he thought, measuring the cliff-edge carefully, drawing closer to it by degrees. At last, at full stretch, he peered over, gazed long at the dark shimmering waves. But then a thought entered his mind: the thought of Oisín roaring for food at home, and a second thought, of the welting he would surely get from his wife if he came home without fish. In an instant his mind was made up, he gripped his rod, freed the hook, put his hand into his pocket and took out the twist of catskin that the old woman had given him. He unwrapped it carefully, and there in his hand was a type of snail, two black eyes looking up at him from the ends of little horns on top of its head. Its body was green, with yellow spots, and Fionn felt his skin beginning to crawl.

'He's the quarest divil I ever saw,' he muttered to himself, not knowing whether to stick the hook in it or not. In the end he did, good and tight, too, but as soon as the metal met the snail Fionn's ears were pierced by a painful 'SqueEEEE!!'

The horns shrivelled up, the eyes disappeared and Fionn dropped the creature in disgust over the edge of the cliff. Down it went, and plop!

into the dark water. Fionn shrugged and readied himself, expecting the rod to be dragged out of his hands and fully determined that any fish taking it would fully earn its feed. He braced himself, left leg to the front, rod over knee, waiting. Nothing happened. He shuffled, changed his stance, right leg to the front. Nothing. In all his days hunting deer, boars, badgers and rabbits he had never experienced anything like this. On every other hunt dogs, trumpets and men barking, braying and shouting would make a man dizzy with delight and so it should be here and now. But nothing was stirring.

After a few minutes of this Fionn scowled, growled, 'Ah, to hell with it! I'll have a puff,' and put the rod under his foot while he rummaged for his pipe and his pouch of buachaláns (ragwort) – there was no tobacco that time. He had just begun to enjoy the ring of smoke circling his head when, without warning, there was a vicious tug on the line and the rod was almost pulled from under his boot.

'O, hanam 'on diabhal, what's here?' he gabbled, dropping his pipe and snatching at the rod. Down, down it went, and Fionn pulled and strained to hold it, but the more he held it back the stronger the pull became. Now, Fionn was no weak man, but slowly, very slowly, he found himself being dragged forward, nearer and nearer to the edge of the cliff. He dug in his heels, but his efforts were idle, a waste of leather, as he could get no grip on the bare rock.

'What'll I do?' he gibbered. 'If I let go my rod 'tis gone for ever' – even the thought of that frightened him because well he knew that if he arrived home with his hands hanging to him, one as long and as empty as the other, his wife would have no sweet welcome for him. She might even go to the black press and beat him over the head with her secret weapon – the breadpin which she spoke of as 'my harmful' in her more loving moments.

'I'd better hang on, whatever happens,' he said.

The words were hardly spoken when the rod jerked down and he was pulled over the edge of the cliff, protesting all the way down. He was still roaring when he hit the water and raised spatters almost to the sky. Down he plunged, shutting his mouth as soon as he tasted the salty water, holding on for dear life to the rod. He had no time to recover even some of his wits because immediately the rod and his hands were yanked out, full stretch, before him, and he was off through the water like a torpedo. Eyes closed, cheeks puffed out, hair streaming

behind him, he was dragged out into the deep and down, always down. Now, Fionn was like most other people in not being able to breathe under water – a big disadvantage here, and spots and bright lights began to appear in the darkness behind his eyelids. He strained, wriggled and began to turn blue, and his life would surely have ended then had not the creature that was pulling the rod decided at that moment to swerve into a dark opening in the seabed. Before Fionn knew anything he was struggling for breath and splashing madly in a large under-water cave.

He grew quiet as his wind came back, and began to look about him. The more he looked, the wider his eyes became. His mouth struggled with words but no words came. He had no clue what kind of place this was for he had seen nothing like it in all his travels. On one side there were three big pillars, bright lamps hanging from chains down between them, and on the other were three steps leading up out of the water and onto a narrow passageway in the rock. Fionn's mouth hung open while his eyes wandered across the scene, only to snap shut with a crack of teeth when he found himself eye-to-eye with a strange-looking creature. Speechless they gazed at each other a moment. Then with a little snarl the creature fixed its attention on its fish-like tail and began to cut and saw with angry strokes. Fionn's eyes followed every move, terror growing in him as he began to understand his position. He saw the long scaly tail and half-body, the woman's face, hands and hair, and somewhere in his mind a memory stirred, an echo of a story he had heard in his youth, a tale of mermaids under the sea. But even as he thought, his eyes were riveted on her hands and the little silver knife she was working with so fiercely. He felt the sudden tug on his line as she flung something from her, and the truth crashed on him like an oak tree falling! He had hooked her tail and only now had she freed herself! Words, explanations crowded each other in his mouth, and he could say nothing. Silently she folded her little knife and turned her eyes on him, cold, deadly eyes. If looks could kill, Fionn would have died at that moment. But she spoke.

'Who are you? What evil chance brought you to this place?'

In his fright he had no answer to make, only a gurgling in his throat like a fish gasping out its life on a riverbank. Her voice rose in anger: 'What did I ever do to you that you offered me this injury? Having my bath in *our* Dark Pool, and to be hooked like that by a skulking stranger like you! What were you doing there at all, up on our cliff?' Raising her voice she shouted, 'Spying on me, were you? Is that what you were at?'

Fionn saw that she was working herself into a fury and that there was no knowing where this situation might end, but that it could only end badly for him. So he mastered his fear and said in his Sunday voice: 'Oh, no! No, your highness. I was—'

'I'm not my highness,' she snapped.

'More's the pity, because you deserve to be,'

he wheedled, and before she could interrupt again he explained: 'Look, I was only trying to get a bit of fish for the young lad at home – Oisín is his name, you know. A very hungry name, too, 'cos he has what milk we ever had drank!'

He noticed that she faltered and seemed to clear her throat, as if trying to think of what to say next.

'Ahem–hem!' she began, 'I don't know do I believe you or not. But I'll bring you to someone who'll make no mistakes. Come on.'

'Hold on a second, now,' blustered Fionn. 'Who might that be?'

'Her highness, our queen. No less! She'll be anxious to see you, too, because many a long day has passed since we saw anyone from the big world above down here. So follow me!'

Fionn had no choice and he knew it. Miserably he trudged up the three steps out of the water, his boots squelching as he went. Already she was waddling ahead at a speed which surprised him and he had to shift himself to catch up to her. Left they went through the narrow passage, right, and left again. All Fionn's hopes of memorising the way disappeared as one turn followed another and at last he resigned himself to chance and to his own strong arm to get him safely out again.

They hurried on, for how long he could not tell, until, without warning, they came to a long, bright hall. Fionn stood dazzled by the sudden burst of light but the mermaid continued on without a pause to the far end where, on a glittering throne, a mermaid sat with a royal air about her. Even from that distance Fionn knew that his journey was at an end, and this was none other than the queen. But something else had caught his attention now. There, standing behind the throne, tails on the ground, fins resting on the shimmering gold, were three of the most villainous-looking fish ever seen, each one showing its huge yellow teeth and seeming to smirk as Fionn faltered at the door.

A short whispered discussion with the queen and Fionn's mermaid returned and said, 'She wants to have words with you.'

Fionn could say nothing, only squelch towards her, his thoughts growing gloomier with every step. The nearer he came the more he could feel the cold fishy eyes boring into him from every side, but there was no going back now. He stood before her, waiting, mannerly, to begin.

'Kneel down there in front of me!' she commanded. He did so, afraid to do otherwise,

knowing that his getting out safely depended on the happenings of the next few minutes.

'Kiss the floor! And don't stop until I tell you!' the queen said.

He did, glad that at least she was talking to him.

'Enough!'

Fionn straightened up, gazed at her.

'Now, explain yourself. And quickly, too!'

From behind the throne the three monstrous fish ogled him, licking their fangs all the while.

'Your highness, I'm not the type of man to steal anything from any person, or to spy on people, either. All I was doing up on the cliff was trying to catch a few sharks for my hungry young lad at home, just like the old woman told me to.'

The word 'sharks' was no sooner out of his mouth when he knew that he had said the wrong thing, for the three monsters behind the throne set up a gnashing and rattling of their teeth that almost deafened him. He cringed, wanting more than anything, now, to turn and run, but held there by the strange look that came over the queen's face. She silenced the three with a wave of her hand.

'Old woman? What old woman?' she asked.

He described the old one he had met at Geata

na Spioraid as accurately as he could, but before he could finish she was murmuring to herself, 'So that's where she got to.'

Then to Fionn she said, 'D'you know what that "nice ould lady" was?'

'Dhera, some ould traveller, I suppose,' said Fionn innocently.

'She was *not!*' snapped the queen, rising from her seat. 'She was no ordinary woman, but a close friend of mine in times past. But jealousy and greed are terrible diseases, and she's a friend no longer.'

Fionn saw the danger that such a personal affair held for him and tried to change the subject slightly.

'Could you be making a mistake, I wonder? This lady, now, she had no. . . ah. . . tail like yours.'

'That honour is reserved only for those who deserve it' – giving his boots a withering look. 'When she was banished from our land and condemned to hobble about the big world above she lost her tail.'

A cloud of gloom settled on Fionn as, more and more with every word she spoke, he realised that he had come to this place in the worst way possible. But he shook himself and said, 'All right. Look! If you let me out of here now I'll go peacefully on my way and I'll come back here no more, or tell anyone what I saw here. Most of all, I won't go fishing any more. I think I'd be better off hunting rabbits, even though I was warned about that by the Good People. There'd be less risk in it than in this fishing thing, anyway, bad luck to it. A fellow'd be better off racing his shadow up and down a hill than standing up on a cliff waiting for the legs to be swept from under him.'

'Racing. . .' said she, stroking her chin with finger and thumb. 'Are you interested in racing?'

'Oh, indeed, many of the best days I ever spent were—'

'That's it, so,' she interrupted. 'A race is what we'll have. You'd like a race, wouldn't you?'

'Begor, I wouldn't mind at all, your highness. But what kind of race had you in your head?' Fionn asked.

'You know the steps where you came up out of the water?' she said.

'I do.'

'You know the cliff you fell down over?' she continued.

'Ha! Will I ever forget it!'

'Well, between those two is the race-course,' she smiled. A mirthless smile. Fionn frowned. A look of puzzlement crossed his face.

'I don't. . .' he began, but he stopped. The truth was beginning to dawn on him. An unpleasant truth.

'What you'll do, now,' she continued, 'is go down those three steps again, into the water and start swimming for the cliff. You'll get ten minutes of a start on my friends here' – turning to smile at each of the three horrors in turn – 'and if you can get to the cliff and climb it before they catch you, well and good.'

'And if I can't?' shouted Fionn.

'Well and bad!' she answered drily.

She clapped her hands. At once Fionn's mermaid returned, bringing a little glass container filled with water. The queen held it, displayed it.

'When I take away my finger from this little hole' – pointing to it – 'the water will drip out. In ten minutes it will be empty. I hope you're well on your way by then,' and she looked at Fionn in amusement.

'Is this the kind of justice ye have here?' thundered Fionn. 'If you think that I'm going to make fun of myself so that you can have a laugh, you have another think coming. I'm not moving from this spot!' and he folded his arms and stamped his boot firmly on the floor.

She lifted her finger from the hole.

'If you want to be eaten here, that's all right,'

she said smoothly, 'but wouldn't you do the tidy thing and jump into the water. There'd be less cleaning up to be done that way.'

'No! What kind of race would that be. They have fins and I haven't. I won't stir!'

'Eight minutes,' she smiled.

The eyes of the three sharks behind the throne were glued to the little jar, with occasional glances at Fionn, as a person might check a joint of meat cooking. He himself began to watch the jar, the water slowly sinking. A cold sweat broke out on his forehead. He began to waver. . . to twitch. He leaped.

'Ah, here! To hell with it,' he rasped, snatching himself away from the silent little group, thundering down the hallway without farewell, shouting over his shoulder at the door, 'And I'll tell everyone where ye are, too. And may ye rot with the plague!'

Without waiting for a reply he blundered into the narrow passageways, ran blindly, and by some miracle found himself at the three steps and the gently-lapping water. No time to admire the place now! Drawing a mighty draught of air into his barrel-chest he leaped from the top step, fishing rod still in his grasp, and began to thresh the water frantically to a foam as he struggled downwards to the mouth of the cave. Finding that the rod hindered his hand-strokes he pushed it under his belt and fixed his mind's eye on the cliff-face which was now his only salvation. In a whirl of beating hands and legs he passed the cave-entrance and broke for the surface as though he might pull chunks from the water itself. But he seemed to have gone a pitifully small distance towards that faraway light when behind him he heard, one after another, three splashes.

'Crom help me now, but they're coming, the dirty devils!' gurgled Fionn. Sure enough, seconds later a rushing sound gathered behind him and in the time it takes to clear a stubborn cough he was surrounded. The three evil-looking beasts swam sleekly around him, more dangerous-looking in the water than ever they had looked out of it, each with longer, sharper teeth than the next, eyes glaring coldly.

Fionn treaded water, his mind working overtime to find a way out of this deadly danger. The sharks nudged each other, jostling for first bite, but eventually the biggest of the three shouldered the others behind him, gathered himself up like a tightened spring for the blood-sweep that would leave Fionn a twisted wreck of eel-meat. In those terrible seconds a coldness that had nothing of the coldness of the water in it settled on Fionn, and out of that shivering terror a vision of a battle-charge by the Shannon water sprang before his mind – forty shrieking warriors of the O'Connors, armed to the eyes, thundering in a herd down on him, swords, axes whirling; he, spitting laughter in their faces, throwing down his shield, left leg set firmly in front of right, grasping spear stiffly, two-handed before him. Oh! The fear in the eyes of the leader as his own rush, his own men hurled him onwards towards that wicked two-handed death. His tortured efforts to stop, his orders ending in a gurgling shriek, the confusion as Fionn jerked back and leaped to the attack, sword in hand now, a new death threatening every attacker as he laughed grimly. They had scattered before his fury, those hard fighting-men, like dust in a door-draught, as he stood smiling, as now he smiled before the charge of this grey killer of the deep. Snatching his rod from his belt he settled his stance, kicking furiously to keep himself upright, and held the rod forward in his iron clutch to meet the shock of shark. Whistling through the water he came, fangs bared for the kill. But he never made contact. Fionn, aiming the point of the rod carefully, guided it straight into the shark's eye, and immediately, 'BLUBLUBLUBLUB' the creature sent up a cloud of bubbles and muffled roaring close to Fionn's face. The sleek fins shot up to the face, but too late! The eye was out. At once he lost all interest in his prey, sank head over tail to the bottom, and groped back home, beaten.

Fionn, having no spare breath to stay and admire his work, was already swimming on, leaving the other two sharks to gaze at their companion and learn a lesson if they had a mind to. But no! Then, as now, intelligence escaped them and they turned once more to their work. Silently they glided up behind him, intent on snapping off his legs. But Fionn's neck-hair tingled to warn him and he slipped sideways just as the leader's jaws tore through water which had contained a leg one second before. Now came the second set of teeth driving at him, but in an instant Fionn had whipped off his long boot and held it straight in the way of the fierce nose and mouth. He was thumped backwards through the water by the force of the impact, but the shark's nose was securely in the boot. And now came a wondrous change in that sleek killer. His colour changed from grey to green to yellow; the sleekness left his skin, and his tail began to flap in wild convulsions as the terrible black contents of Fionn's boot did their evil work on his senses. Suddenly the threshing body shuddered, stiffened, turned over and sank slowly to the sea-floor.

Fionn was beginning to feel the lack of breath uncomfortably and was swimming again. But in an instant his way was barred by the fearsome fangs of the last shark. Determined not to make the same mistakes as its friends, and thinking to frighten Fionn to death, it stopped two feet from his face, opened its mouth and showed every tooth in a huge snarl.

'Begob, what an ugly gob,' bubbled Fionn, and without another thought opened his own mouth in a leer that was even more horrible – because Fionn had only four teeth, like the upright bars of a gate, from all the many battle-blows down the years. Now it was the turn of the shark to pause, its eyes out on stalks with fright, and in that lull Fionn's fingers groped under its lower jaw and began to tickle.

The cruel jaws closed in a smile. The evil eyes danced with mirth, and, 'Pahahu-gluglug', a spurt of bubbles told of its great enjoyment of this friendly gesture. But on the other side of the bubbles Fionn was collecting his strength for the final say in the matter. While his fingers still tickled the shark into lunatic guffaws his other hand streaked forward, connected like a hammer, and where there were rows of gleaming fangs a moment before there was now only a gaping hole in the shark's face and splinters spreading to the four corners of the ocean floor.

Without a pause to look, Fionn, his head spinning from lack of air, rushed for the cliff-face, reached it, climbed it as if there were ladders on it, and sat panting feverishly on top.

How long he might have sat there he could not tell. The dark waters below held his attention and he stared. It was a seagull snatching at his outspread fingers on the rock that snapped him back to sense.

'Hanam 'on diabhal!' he cried gathering himself, 'I'll be killed! The day is gone and I should be at home a long time ago.'

He hurried back along the path he had travelled that morning, one foot still squelching in its boot, the other silent. Fionn hardly noticed, so intent was he on putting the road behind him.

He had travelled most of the way, was nearing Geata na Spioraid, when before him he saw a dark bent figure. It saw him at the same time and at once turned and hobbled back the way it had come. But too late! In six strides Fionn had caught up, and there, glaring at him was none other than the old woman.

''Tis. . . 'tis early you're back,' she stuttered, hiding something inside her shawl.

'And no thanks to you, either,' snarled Fionn. 'And I'll talk to you about that, too, in a minute. But first, what did I see you hiding there under that shawl? Come on! Out with it!'

'That's nothing at all to do with you', she squealed, fright in her voice.

'We'll see about that,' he grated, catching her hand, pulling it from inside the shawl. There exposed, her long nails circling it tightly, was a leather money-bag.

'O, you thing, you! You evil ould cailleach (old hag)!' he roared, anger in every word but fear too, now, because he recognised the bag. It was the same that he kept in the little hole near the fireplece at home, the same that contained his gold that would supply the family with heat and light during the dark winter. And now, at the thought of what the old hag had done – robbed his house, maybe killed his wife and Oisín – he was filled with a great rage. Snatching the bag in his left hand he hardly heard her shouting, 'Aeee! My nails! Them nails took a lifetime to grow, and you're after breaking every one of them!'

'I'll break more than them!' he shouted, and as though in the grip of a fierce nightmare his right hand tightened around her neck, lifted, and flung her into the air. Off she streaked through the sky like a shooting star or some misguided missile, and was never seen in those parts again.

Mouth open, Fionn ran and ran for home. He cleared the outer wall of the yard in his stride, screeched to a halt at the door and toppled in.

As he picked himself up he heard Oisín's hungry bellowing and a tidal wave of relief and delight swept over him. He staggered to the cradle and looked lovingly at the child's face, bloated now from crying. Then a sound on the stairs made him wheel round, to see his wife advancing in her nightgown down the stairs, pale as any ghost. She paused.

'Well? Did you bring it?' she asked.

'It? Did I – oh, yes. Here it is in my hand' – lifting the purse. 'I got it back safe an' sound.' There was pride in his voice.

'What are you talking about?' said she, advancing threateningly down the steps.

'Our money,' he smiled toothily.

'Money? What ould gibberish is this? Where's the fish for the child?'

She had reached the bottom step.

Fionn stood as if struck by a battle-axe. His mind clicked back to the reality of the situation.

'Oh? The fish. . . Well, I'll tell you, now. . .'

She saw that all he had to offer was excuses, and like lightning she was at the door of the black press, sickness or no sickness. But Fionn was even quicker. Before she could open the fatal door his hand was on the latch and he was pleading.

'No! Anything but that! Look, didn't I bring back our gold' – holding the bag for her to see – 'What more do you want?'

A strange look came into her face as she looked at the bag.

'You dirty ould amadán (*fool*)! That isn't our

money-bag at all!'

'Hah! Are you out of your mind? Are you saying that I don't know my own purse? Don't I count that gold twice every day, so why wouldn't I know it?'

'I don't care! That's not your purse. Look at the bottom of it, will you.'

He did, and there he saw a mark that was strange to him. With a troubled look beginning to cloud his face he looked at her again, turned and rushed to the hole by the fireplace. There he drew out – none other than his own purse, just as he had left it.

'Crom be good to me!' he groaned, looking from one purse to the other, 'but I attacked the wrong woman!'

'Never mind that now,' threatened his wife. 'What are you going to do about feeding the child there?'

'Oh! I'll go this very minute to Mac Giolla Meidhre of Gleann Draoi. He has grand Kerry cows for sale, the best milkers in the country, and I'll buy them, as many as we need, with this new gold.'

'All right, but don't come home without at least six of them. That way, maybe we'll have some drop to drink ourselves as well as the fellow there in the cradle.'

Fionn went, glad to escape without injury to pride or head. He made his bargain with Mac Giolla Meidhre for six black cows, paid his cash down, gathered them up, three under each arm, and strode home with them bellowing with terror.

'Now,' he said to his wife, 'we should have no more bother with himself there,' pointing to Oisín.

That was how it was. From that day on there was peace in the house and Oisín grew up to be handsome, good-natured and wise. And all because of the milk of those Kerry cows and the journey of Fionn to the land of the mermaids.

More Interesting Books

A SPOOKY IRISH TALE FOR CHILDREN

EDDIE LENIHAN

Before the coming of a dark stranger from Thurginia in Germany, pictures had never been painted in Ireland. The artist is welcomed even in the royal palace of Tara, where he decorates the walls of every room. But in return for this amazing new craft a high price is demanded: a series of gruesome killings that are carried out within the royal palace itself. Taoscán Mac Liath, the high king's chief druid and the wisest man in the land is puzzled, but he finds out enough to realise that if something is not done – and quickly – there will be few people left to enjoy the beautiful paintings. He enlists the help of Fionn Mac Cumhail to solve the eerie and terrible mystery.

STRANGE IRISH TALES FOR CHILDREN

EDDIE LENIHAN

Strange Irish Tales for Children is a collection of four exciting stories, by seanchaí Edmund Lenihan, which will entertain and amuse children of all ages. The stories tell of the hair-raising adventures of the Fianna and of their fighting and hunting – 'How the Blackbird came to Ireland', 'The Strange Case of Seán na Súl, 'Taoscán MacLiath and the Magic Bees' and 'Fionn MacCumhail and the Making of the Burren'.